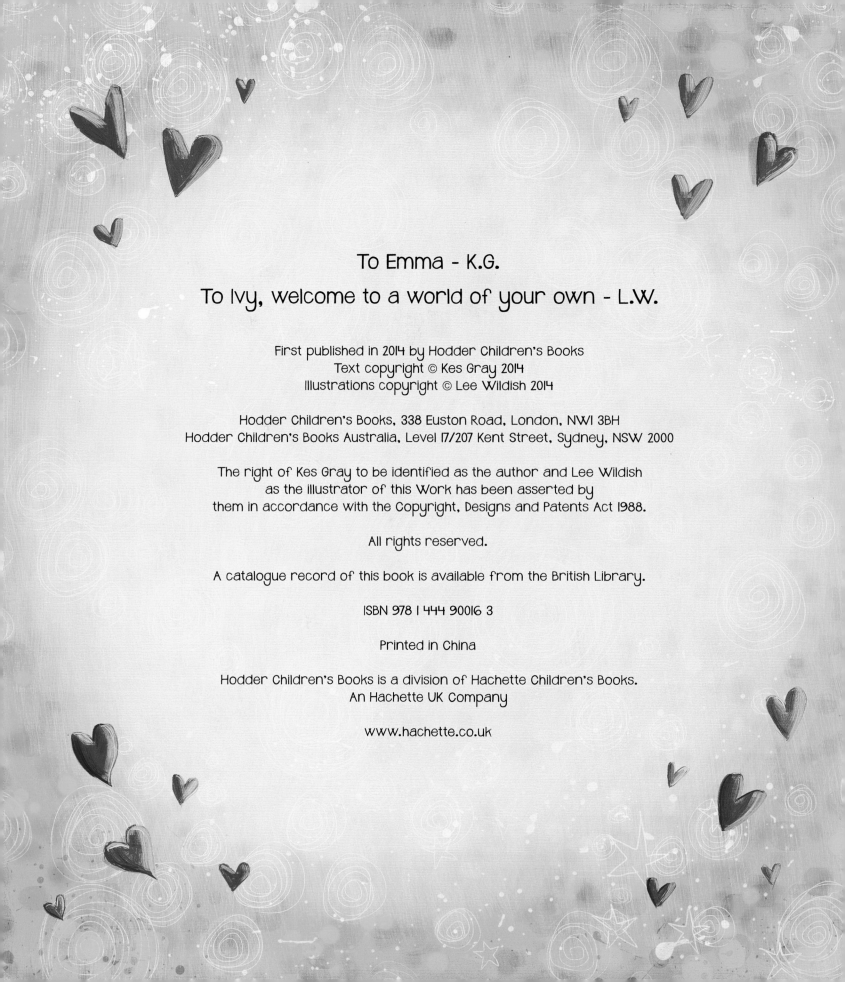

To Emma - K.G.

To Ivy, welcome to a world of your own - L.W.

First published in 2014 by Hodder Children's Books
Text copyright © Kes Gray 2014
Illustrations copyright © Lee Wildish 2014

Hodder Children's Books, 338 Euston Road, London, NW1 3BH
Hodder Children's Books Australia, Level 17/207 Kent Street, Sydney, NSW 2000

The right of Kes Gray to be identified as the author and Lee Wildish
as the illustrator of this Work has been asserted by
them in accordance with the Copyright, Designs and Patents Act 1988.

A catalogue record of this book is available from the British Library.

ISBN 978 1 444 90016 3

Printed in China

Hodder Children's Books is a division of Hachette Children's Books.
An Hachette UK Company

www.hachette.co.uk

WORRIES GO AWAY!

Kes Gray & Lee Wildish

Hodder
Children's
Books

A division of Hachette Children's Books

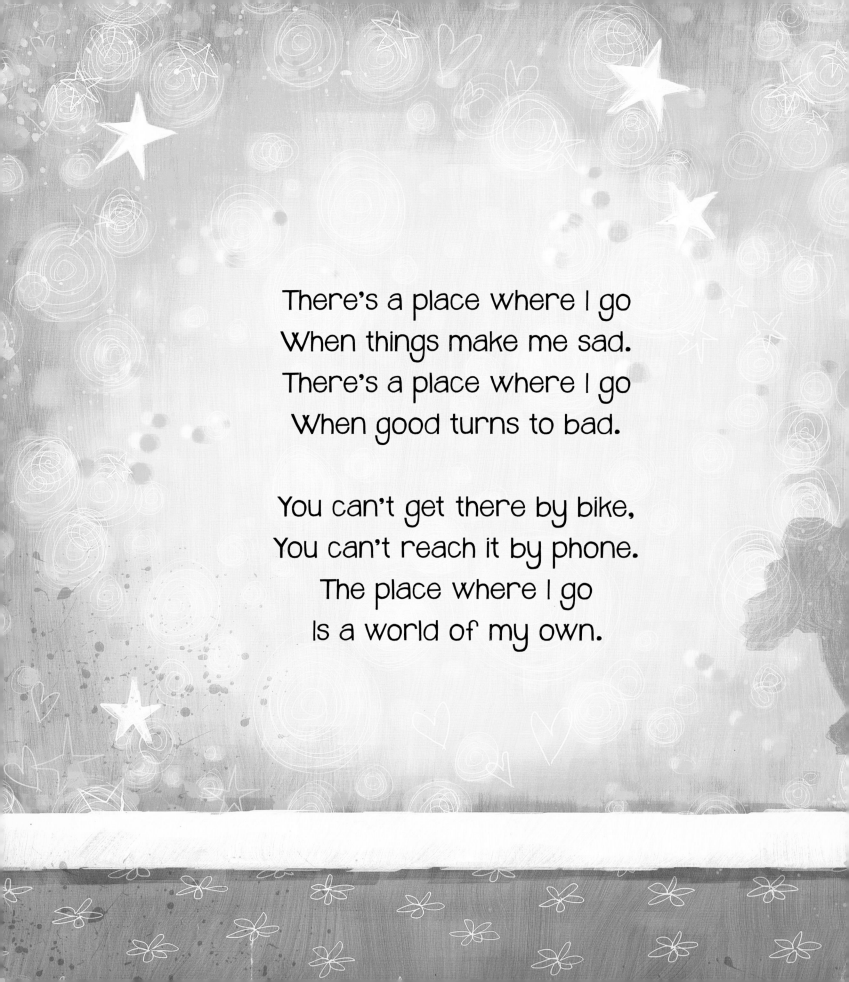

There's a place where I go
When things make me sad.
There's a place where I go
When good turns to bad.

You can't get there by bike,
You can't reach it by phone.
The place where I go
Is a world of my own.

A world of my own
Is inside my head
Where no one can reach me,
Where no words are said.

In a world of my own
There's no one but me.
It's the place I escape to,
It's the place I feel free.

At first when I get there
There are flowers and trees,
There's birdsong and blue sky,
There's honey and bees.

There are cream cakes to eat
And there's cola to drink.
There are benches to sit on and places to think.

It's pretty near perfect.
There's fun to be had,
But after a while it begins to feel bad...

The worries I take here
Begin to take hold.
They give me the shivers,
They make me feel cold.

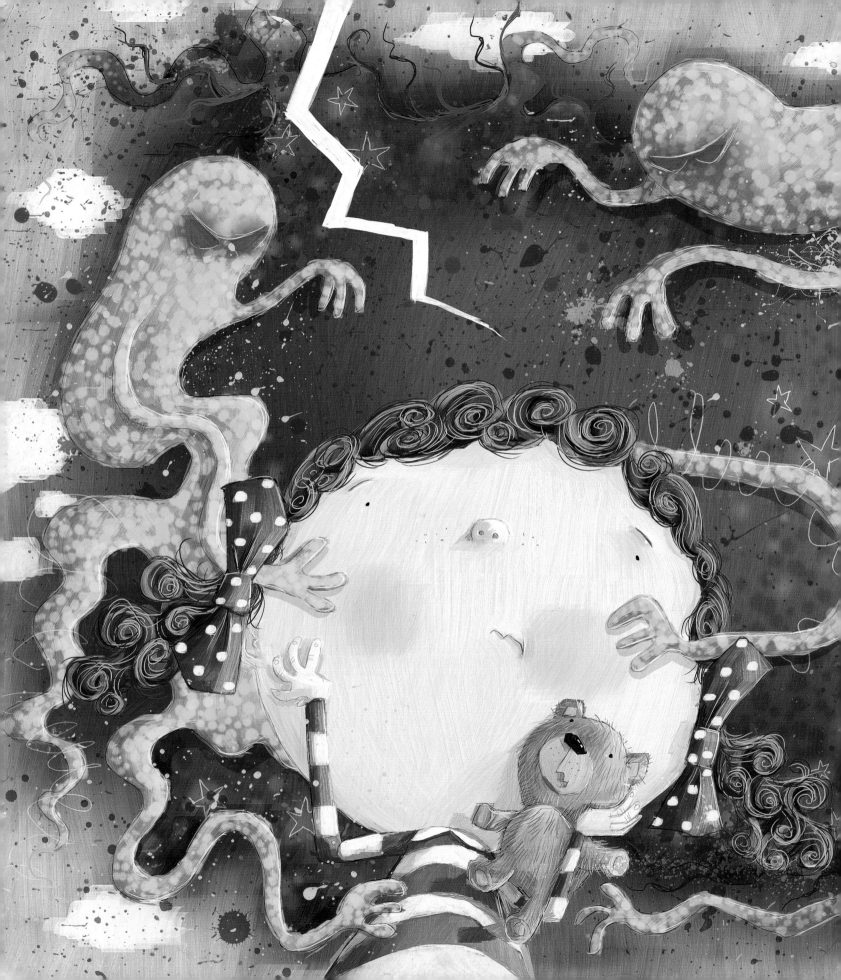

My worries grow larger,
They play on my mind.
They start to play tricks
Of the scariest kind.

They turn into monsters
That circle and prowl,
That bellow and cackle,
That grizzle and growl.

The blue sky above me
Turns black as deep space.
I turn and I run,
But the worries give chase.

They won't let me lose them,
They won't let me go.

I'm beginning to panic,
I'm starting to slow.

I stagger, I stumble,
I trip and I fall.
I climb to my feet
with my back to a wall.

My fingers feel something –
Four panels or more,
Two hinges, a handle –
It feels like a door!

There's a door in the darkness!
It's too black to see.

It's a door with a keyhole,
Minus the key.

I peer through the keyhole, my eyes open wide.
People who love me are gathered outside.

They've been trying to reach me.
They've knocked and they've knocked,
But the door to my world
Has always been locked.

I stare at the door,
The door stares at me.
Suddenly I realise

I AM THE KEY!

If I open my heart
To my family and friends
My worries might go
And my troubles might end.

I turn the door handle
And push from my side.

My world fills with light
As the door opens wide.

Fingers reach forward
To ruffle my hair,
I'm greeted with kindness
by people who care.

I feel so much better,
Not lonely or down.
And as for my worries?
They've upped and left town!

The next time I'm troubled,
There's a place I will go.
Not a world of my own.
But to someone I know.